The DRAMA LLAMA

Rachel Morrisroe & Ella Okstad

PUFFIN

For Alex. Thank you for always taming my llamas. I love you. – R.M.

For my boys: HC, PA and OJ – E.O.

PUFFIN BOOKS
UK | USA | Canada | Ireland | Australia | India | New Zealand | South Africa
Puffin Books is part of the Penguin Random House group of companies whose addresses can be found at global.penguinrandomhouse.com.

www.penguin.co.uk www.puffin.co.uk www.ladybird.co.uk

First published 2022
001

Printed in China
ISBN: 978–0–241–45300–1

The authorized representative in the EEA is Penguin Random House Ireland, Morrison Chambers, 32 Nassau Street, Dublin D02 YH68

A CIP catalogue record for this book is available from the British Library

All correspondence to: Puffin Books, Penguin Random House Children's, One Embassy Gardens, 8 Viaduct Gardens, London SW11 7BW

Alex Allen's brain was very curious indeed.
It worked as fast as lightning, at near supersonic speed.
Whenever Alex worried, it would really take its toll,
as that's when something happened that was out of his control . . .

It happened during class
when Alex didn't know the answer . . .

It happened
at a party
when he wasn't
the best
dancer . . .

It happened
with his sister
when they had
a LITTLE fall out . . .

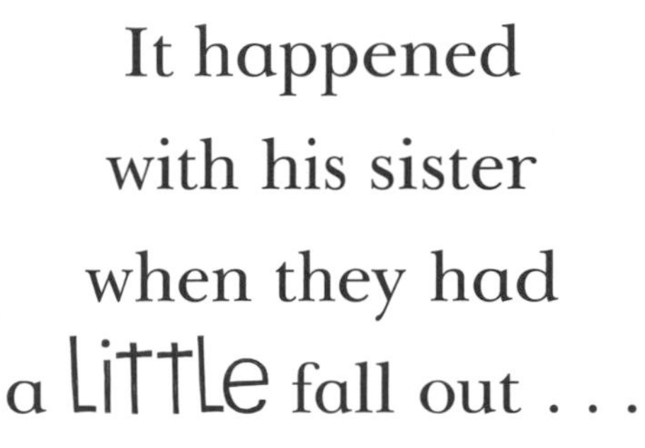

It happened during football
when he tripped and kicked the ball out.

Whenever he was worried
or whenever there was drama,
Alex Allen's brain produced . . .

... A LIVING
BREATHING

LLAMA!

One wild and windy sports day, Alex thought, "What if I slip?
This egg is very wobbly and I'm worried I might trip!"

That's when as plain as daylight
on that dismal afternoon . . .

a LLAMA hurtled round the track . . .

. . . and won

the

egg-and-spoon!

Now, usually his llama disappeared within the day,
but on that fateful afternoon it didn't go away.

It skipped around the supermarket, knocking down the beans.
It licked the lemon buns and turned its nose up at the greens.

"Distract it with the doughnuts," Mum said. "Maybe just ignore it?
Perhaps if we both scarper we can get back home before it?"

Running was quite useless because – like a pongy smell –
all the places Alex went, the llama went as well.

As Alex worried more, that's when the llama started growing.
It jumped into his bathwater, which started overflowing.

Bedtime was a **nightmare** –
Alex kept on counting sheep.
A llama in pyjamas makes it
very hard to sleep!

Alex tried his hardest to forget about his worry,
but llamas can be hard to lose in any kind of hurry.

He played a game of
hide-and-seek . . .

He left it on a train . . .

Like llama-shaped eLastic,

it just pinged straight back again.

He tied it to an apple tree . . .

He locked it in a zoo . . .

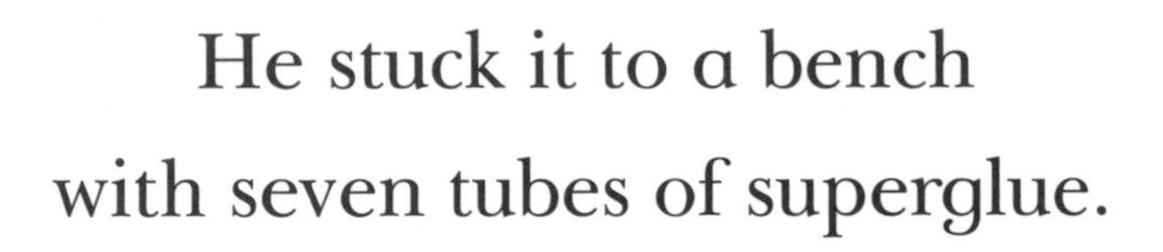

He stuck it to a bench
with seven tubes of superglue.

He posted it to Panama . . .

He locked it in the attic . . .

The more he tried to lose the thing, the more it got dramatic.

He walked it through some fresh cement to glue it in the MUCK . . .

But when it found him back at school
things really came UNSTUCK!

The llama was now totally and utterly ginormous.
It squeezed into the classroom –
as the teacher looked on, gormless.

It thundered round the library,
knocking bookshelves here
and there.

It munched up half the books
and then it chewed Ms Myrtle's hair!

The llama really started causing panic and hysteria,
chasing kids and lunchtime helpers
round the cafeteria.

Taming it was useless –
it was terrible at sitting.
And pretty soon it all got worse . . .

THE LLAMA

STARTED
SPITTING!

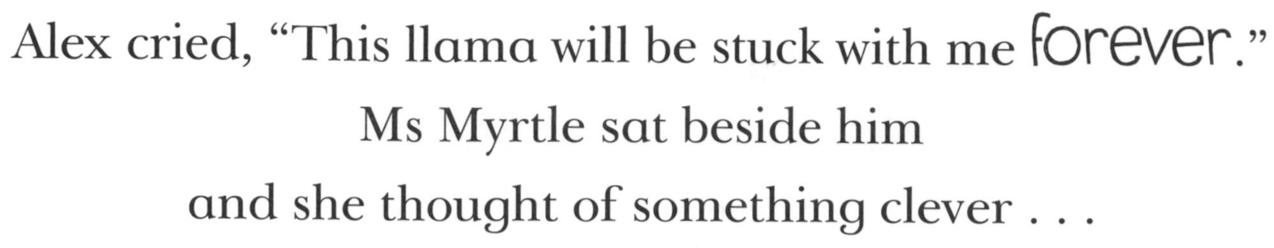

Alex cried, "This llama will be stuck with me forever."
Ms Myrtle sat beside him
and she thought of something clever . . .

The teacher spoke (the llama
paused from gobbling the grass).
"Sometimes . . ." she said, "these feelings
take a longer time to pass.

See, everyone feels worried – it's OK to feel upset.
And caring for your feelings can be easy to forget.

When a fear or worry starts to leave you feeling stressed,
find someone to talk to because talking is the best."

As Alex told her all the things
that left him in a MUDDLE,

the giant llama halved in size . . .
. . . and scooped him in a cuddle.

Alex felt much happier and stronger from that day.
Sometimes the llama stays a while, sometimes it goes away.

But when the llama grows
in size or starts to misbehave . . .

then Alex Allen tries his best to
practise something brave.

For talking to a trusted person
makes the creature calmer,
and helps to make life easier. . .

. . . when living with

A LLAMA!